HIGH HORSE RAMPAGE
(GENTS ON THE RAMPAGE)

BY

ROBERT E. HOWARD

British Library Cataloguing-in-Publication Data
A catalogue record for this book is available from the
British Library

Robert E. Howard

Robert Ervin Howard was born in Peaster, Texas in 1906. During his youth, his family moved between a variety of Texan boomtowns, and Howard – a bookish and somewhat introverted child – was steeped in the violent myths and legends of the Old South. Although he loved reading and learning, Howard developed a distinctly Texan, hardboiled outlook on the world. He became a passionate fan of boxing, taking it up at an amateur level, and from the age of nine began to write adventure tales of semi-historical bloodshed. In 1919, when Howard was thirteen, his family moved to the Central Texas hamlet of Cross Plains, where he would stay for the rest of his life.

At fifteen Howard began to read the pulp magazines of the day, and to write more seriously. The December 1922 issue of his high school newspaper featured two of his stories, 'Golden Hope Christmas' and 'West is West'. In 1924 he sold his first piece – a short caveman tale titled 'Spear and Fang' – for $16 to the not-yet-famous *Weird Tales* magazine. He published with the magazine regularly over the next few years. 1929 was a breakout year for Howard, in that the 23-year-old writer began to sell to other magazines, such as *Ghost Stories* and *Argosy*, both of whom had previously sent him hundreds of rejection slips. In 1930, he began a correspondence with weird fiction master H. P. Lovecraft which ran up to his death six years later, and is regarded as one of the great correspondence cycles in all of fantasy literature.

It was partly due to Lovecraft's encouragement that Howard created his most famous character, Conan the Cimmerian. Conan – a barbarian-turned-King during the Hyborian Age, a mythical period of some 12,000 years ago – featured in seventeen *Weird Tales* stories between 1933 and 1936, and is now regarded as having spawned the 'sword and sorcery' genre, making Howard's influence on fantasy literature comparable to that of J. R. R. Tolkien's. The Conan stories have since been adapted many times, most famously in the series of films starring Arnold Schwarzenegger.

Howard was enjoying an all-time high in sales by the beginning of 1936, but he was also deeply upset by the ill health of his mother, who had fallen into a coma. On the morning of June 11, 1936, he asked an attending nurse whether she would ever recover, and the nurse replied negatively. Howard walked to his car, parked outside the family home in Cross Plains, and shot himself. He died eight hours later, aged just thirty.

I GOT A LETTER FROM Aunt Saragosa Grimes the other day which said:

Dear Breckinridge:

I believe time is softenin' yore Cousin Bearfield Buckner's feelings toward you. He was over here to supper the other night jest after he shot the three Evans boys, and he was in the best humor I seen him in since he got back from Colorado. So I jest kind of casually mentioned you and he didn't turn near as purple as he used to every time he heered yore name mentioned. He jest kind of got a little green around the years, and that might of been on account of him chokin on the b'ar meat he was eatin'. And all he said was he was going to beat yore brains out with a post oak maul if he ever ketched up with you, which is the mildest remark he's made about you since he got back to Texas. I believe he's practically give up the idee of sculpin' you alive and leavin' you on the prairie for the buzzards with both laigs broke like he used to swear was his sole ambition. I believe in a year or so it would be safe for you to meet dear Cousin Bearfield, and if you do have to shoot him, I hope you'll be broad-minded and shoot him in some place which ain't vital because after all you know it was yore fault to begin with. We air all well and nothin's happened to speak of except Joe Allison got a arm broke argyin' politics with Cousin Bearfield. Hopin' you air the same, I begs to remane.

3

Yore lovin' Ant Saragosa.

It's heartening to know a man's kin is thinking kindly of him and forgetting petty grudges. But I can see that Bearfield is been misrepresenting things and pizening Aunt Saragosa's mind agen me, otherwise she wouldn't of made that there remark about it being my fault. All fair-minded men knows that what happened warn't my fault--that is all except Bearfield, and he's naturally prejudiced, because most of it happened to him.

I knowed Bearfield was somewheres in Colorado when I j'ined up with Old Man Brant Mulholland to make a cattle drive from the Pecos to the Platte, but that didn't have nothing to do with it. I expects to run into Bearfield almost any place where the licker is red and the shotguns is sawed-offs. He's a liar when he says I come into the High Horse country a-purpose to wreck his life and ruin his career.

Everything I done to him was in kindness and kindredly affection. But he ain't got no gratitude. When I think of the javelina meat I et and the bare-footed bandits I had to associate with whilst living in Old Mexico to avoid having to kill that wuthless critter, his present attitude embitters me.

I never had no notion of visiting High Horse in the first place. But we run out of grub a few miles north of there, so what does Old Man Mulholland do but rout me outa my blankets before daylight, and says, "I want you to take the chuck wagon to High Horse and buy some grub. Here's fifty bucks. If you spends a penny of that for anything but bacon, beans, flour, salt and coffee, I'll have yore life, big as you be."

"Why'n't you send the cook?" I demanded.

"He's layin' helpless in a chaparral thicket reekin' with the fumes of vaniller extract," says Old Man Mulholland. "Anyway, yo're responsible for this famine. But for yore inhuman appetite we'd of had enough grub to last the whole drive. Git goin'. Yo're the only man in the string I trust with money and I don't trust you no further'n I can heave a bull by the tail."

Us Elkinses is sensitive about sech remarks, but Old Man Mulholland was born with a conviction that everybody is out to swindle him, so I maintained a dignerfied silence outside of telling him to go to hell, and harnessed the mules to the chuck wagon and headed for Antioch. I led Cap'n Kidd behind the wagon because I knowed if I left him unguarded he'd kill every he-hoss in the camp before I got back.

Well, jest as I come to the forks where the trail to Gallego splits off of the High Horse road, I heard somebody behind me thumping a banjer and singing, "Oh, Nora he did build the Ark!" So I pulled up and purty soon around the bend come the derndest looking rig I'd saw since the circus come to War Paint.

It was a buggy all painted red, white and blue and drawed by a couple of wall-eyed pintos. And they was a

5

feller in it with a long-tailed coat and a plug hat and fancy checked vest, and a cross-eyed nigger playing a banjer, with a monkey setting on his shoulder.

The white man taken off his plug hat and made me a bow, and says, "Greetings, my mastodonic friend! Can you inform me which of these roads leads to the fair city of High Horse?"

"That's leadin' south," I says. "T'other'n goes east to Gallego. Air you all part of a circus?"

"I resents the implication," says he. "In me you behold the greatest friend to humanity since the inventor of corn licker. I am Professor Horace J. Lattimer, inventor and sole distributor of that boon to suffering humanity, Lattimer's Lenitive Loco Elixir, good for man or beast!"

He then h'isted a jug out from under the seat and showed it to me and a young feller which had jest rode up along the road from Gallego.

"A sure cure," says he. "Have you a hoss which has nibbled the seductive loco-weed? That huge brute you've got tied to the end-gate there looks remarkable wild in his eye, now--"

"He ain't loco," I says. "He's jest blood-thirsty."

"Then I bid you both a very good day, sirs," says he. "I must be on my way to allay the sufferings of mankind. I trust we shall meet in High Horse."

So he drove on, and I started to cluck to the mules, when the young feller from Gallego, which had been eying me very close, he says, "Ain't you Breckinridge Elkins?"

When I says I was, he says with some bitterness, "That there perfessor don't have to go to High Horse to find locoed critters. They's a man in Gallego right now, crazy as a bedbug--yore own cousin, Bearfield Buckner!"

"What?" says I with a vi'lent start, because they hadn't never been no insanity in the family before, only Bearfield's great-grand-uncle Esau who onst voted agen Hickory Jackson. But he recovered before the next election.

"It's the truth," says the young feller. "He's sufferin' from a hallucination that he's goin' to marry a gal over to High Horse by the name of Ann Wilkins. They ain't even no gal by that name there. He was havin' a fit in the saloon when I left, me not bearin' to look on the rooins of a onst noble character. I'm feared he'll do hisself a injury if he ain't restrained."

"Hell's fire!" I said in great agitation. "Is this the truth?"

"True as my name's Lem Campbell," he declared. "I thought bein' as how yo're a relation of his'n, if you could kinda git him out to my cabin a few miles south of Gallego, and keep him there a few days maybe he might git his mind back--"

"I'll do better'n that," I says, jumping out of the wagon and tying the mules. "Foller me," I says, forking Cap'n Kidd. The Perfessor's buggy was jest going out of sight around a bend, and I lit out after it. I was well ahead of Lem Campbell when I overtaken it. I pulled up beside it in a cloud of dust and demanded, "You say that stuff kyores man or beast?"

"Absolutely!" declared Lattimer.

"Well, turn around and head for Gallego," I said. "I got you a patient."

"But Gallego is but a small inland village" he demurs. "There is a railroad and many saloons at High Horse and--"

"With a human reason at stake you sets and maunders about railroads!" I roared, drawing a .45 and impulsively shooting a few buttons off of his coat. "I buys yore whole load of loco licker. Turn around and head for Gallego."

"I wouldn't think of argying," says he, turning pale. "Meshak, don't you hear the gentleman? Get out from under that seat and turn these hosses around."

"Yes suh!" says Meshak, and they swung around jest as Lem Campbell galloped up.

I hauled out the wad Old Man Mulholland gimme and says to him, "Take this dough on to High Horse and buy some grub and have it sent out to Old Man Mulholland's cow camp on the Little Yankton. I'm goin' to Gallego and I'll need the wagon to lug Cousin Bearfield in."

"I'll take the grub out myself," he declared, grabbing the wad. "I knowed I could depend on you as soon as I seen you."

So he told me how to get to his cabin, and then lit out for High Horse and I headed back up the trail. When I passed the buggy I hollered, "Foller me into Gallego. One of you drive the chuck wagon which is standin' at the forks. And don't try to shake me as soon as I git out of sight, neither!"

"I wouldn't think of such a thing," says Lattimer with a slight shudder. "Go ahead and fear not. We'll follow you as fast as we can."

So I dusted the trail for Gallego.

It warn't much of a town, with only jest one saloon, and as I rode in I heard a beller in the saloon and the door flew open and three or four fellows come sailing out on their heads and picked theirselves up and tore out up the street.

"Yes," I says to myself, "Cousin Bearfield is in town, all right."

GALLEGO LOOKED ABOUT like any town does when Bearfield is celebrating. The stores had their doors locked and the shutters up, nobody was on the streets, and off down acrost the flat I seen a man which I taken to be the sheriff spurring his hoss for the hills. I tied Cap'n Kidd to the hitch-rail and as I approached the saloon I nearly fell over a feller which was crawling around on his all-fours with a bartender's apron on and both eyes swelled shet.

"Don't shoot!" says he. "I give up!"

"What happened?" I ast.

"The last thing I remember is tellin' a feller named Buckner that the Democratic platform was silly," says he. "Then I think the roof must of fell in or somethin'. Surely one man couldn't of did all this to me."

"You don't know my cousin Bearfield," I assured him as I stepped over him and went through the door which was tore off its hinges. I'd begun to think that maybe Lem Campbell had exaggerated about Bearfield; he seemed to be acting in jest his ordinary normal manner. But a instant later I changed my mind.

Bearfield was standing at the bar in solitary grandeur, pouring hisself a drink, and he was wearing the damnedest-looking red, yaller, green and purple shirt ever I seen in my life.

"What," I demanded in horror, "is that thing you got on?"

"If yo're referrin' to my shirt," he retorted with irritation, "it's the classiest piece of goods I could find in Denver. I bought it special for my weddin'."

"It's true!" I moaned. "He's crazy as hell."

I knowed no sane man would wear a shirt like that.

"What's crazy about gittin' married?" he snarled, biting the neck off of a bottle and taking a big snort. "Folks does it every day."

I walked around him cautious, sizing him up and down, which seemed to exasperate him considerable.

"What the hell's the matter with you?" he roared, hitching his harness for'ard. "I got a good mind to--"

"Be ca'm, Cousin Bearfield," I soothed him. "Who's this gal you imagine yo're goin' to marry?"

"I don't imagine nothin' about it, you ignerant ape," he retorts cantankerously. "Her name's Ann Wilkins and she lives in High Horse. I'm ridin' over there right away and we gits hitched today."

I shaken my head mournful and said, "You must of inherited this from yore great-grand-uncle Esau. Pap's always said Esau's insanity might crop out in the Buckners again some time. But don't worry. Esau was kyored and voted a straight Democratic ticket the rest of his life. You can be kyored too, Bearfield, and I'm here to do it. Come with me, Bearfield," I says, getting a good rassling grip on his neck.

"Consarn it!" says Cousin Bearfield, and went into action.

We went to the floor together and started rolling in the general direction of the back door and every time he come up on top he'd bang my head agen the floor which soon became very irksome. However, about the tenth revolution I come up on top and pried my thumb out of his teeth and said, "Bearfield, I don't want to have to use force with you,

11

but--ulp!" That was account of him kicking me in the back of the neck.

My motives was of the loftiest, and they warn't no use in the saloon owner belly-aching the way he done afterwards. Was it my fault if Bearfield missed me with a five-gallon demijohn and busted the mirror behind the bar? Could I help it if Bearfield wrecked the billiard table when I knocked him through it? As for the stove which got busted, all I got to say is that self-preservation is the first law of nature. If I hadn't hit Bearfield with the stove he would of ondoubtedly scrambled my features with that busted beer mug he was trying to use like brass knucks.

I'VE HEARD MANIACS fight awful, but I dunno as Bearfield fit any different than usual. He hadn't forgot his old trick of hooking his spur in my neck whilst we was rolling around on the floor, and when he knocked me down with the roulette wheel and started jumping on me with both feet I thought for a minute I was going to weaken. But the shame of having a maniac in the family revived me and I throwed him off and riz and tore up a section of the brass foot-rail and wrapped it around his head. Cousin Bearfield dropped the bowie he'd jest drawed, and collapsed.

I wiped the blood off of my face and discovered I could still see outa one eye. I pried the brass rail off of Cousin Bearfield's head and dragged him out onto the porch by a hind laig, jest as Perfessor Lattimer drove up in his buggy.

Meshak was behind him in the chuck wagon with the monkey, and his eyes was as big and white as saucers.

"Where's the patient?" ast Lattimer, and I said, "This here's him! Throw me a rope outa that wagon. We takes him to Lem Campbell's cabin where we can dose him till he recovers his reason."

Quite a crowd gathered whilst I was tying him up, and I don't believe Cousin Bearfield had many friends in Gallego by the remarks they made. When I lifted his limp carcass up into the wagon one of 'em ast me if I was a law. And when I said I warn't, purty short, he says to the crowd, "Why, hell, then, boys, what's to keep us from payin' Buckner back for all the lickin's he's give us? I tell you, it's our chance! He's unconscious and tied up, and this here feller ain't no sheriff."

"Git a rope!" howled somebody. "We'll hang 'em."

They begun to surge for'ards, and Lattimer and Meshak was so scairt they couldn't hardly hold the lines. But I mounted my hoss and pulled my pistols and says. "Meshak, swing that chuck wagon and head south. Perfessor, you foller him. Hey, you, git away from them mules!"

One of the crowd had tried to grab their bridles and stop 'em, so I shot a heel off'n his boot and he fell down hollering bloody murder.

"Git outa the way!" I bellered, swinging my pistols on the crowd, and they give back in a hurry. "Git goin'," I says, firing some shots under the mules' feet to encourage 'em, and the chuck wagon went out of Gallego jumping and bouncing with Meshak holding onto the seat and hollering blue ruin, and the Perfessor come right behind it in his buggy. I follered the Perfessor looking back to see nobody didn't shoot me in the back, because several men had drawed their pistols. But nobody fired till I was out of good pistol range. Then somebody let loose with a buffalo rifle, but he missed me by at least a foot, so I paid no attention to it, and we was soon out of sight of the town.

I was a feared Bearfield might come to and scare the mules with his bellering, but that brass rail must of been harder'n I thought. He was still unconscious when we pulled up to the cabin which stood in a little wooded cove amongst the hills a few miles south of Gallego. I told Meshak to onhitch the mules and turn 'em into the corral whilst I carried Bearfield into the cabin and laid him on a bunk. I told Lattimer to bring in all the elixir he had, and he brung ten gallons in one-gallon jugs. I give him all the money I had to pay for it.

Purty soon Bearfield come to and he raised his head and looked at Perfessor Lattimer setting on the bunk opposite him in his long tailed coat and plug hat, the cross-eyed nigger and the monkey setting beside him. Bearfield batted his eyes and says, "My God, I must be crazy. That can't be real!"

"Sure, yo're crazy, Cousin Bearfield," I soothed him. "But don't worry. We're goin' to kyore you--"

Bearfield here interrupted me with a yell that turned Meshak the color of a fish's belly.

"Untie me, you son of Perdition!" he roared, heaving and flopping on the bunk like a python with the belly-ache, straining agen his ropes till the veins knotted blue on his temples. "I oughta be in High Horse right now gittin' married--"

"See there?" I sighed to Lattimer. "It's a sad case. We better start dosin' him right away. Git a drenchin' horn. What size dose do you give?"

"A quart at a shot for a hoss," he says doubtfully. "But--"

"We'll start out with that," I says. "We can increase the size of the dose if we need to."

IGNORING BEARFIELD'S terrible remarks I was jest twisting the cork out of a jug when I heard somebody say, "What the hell air you doin' in my shack?"

I turned around and seen a bow-legged critter with drooping whiskers glaring at me kinda pop-eyed from the door.

"What you mean, yore shack?" I demanded, irritated at the interruption. "This shack belongs to a friend of mine which has lent it to us."

"Yo're drunk or crazy," says he, clutching at his whiskers convulsively. "Will you git out peaceable or does I have to git vi'lent?"

"Oh, a cussed claim-jumper, hey?" I snorted, taken his gun away from him when he drawed it. But he pulled a bowie so I throwed him out of the shack and shot into the dust around him a few times jest for warning.

"I'll git even with you, you big lummox!" he howled, as he ran for a scrawny looking sorrel he had tied to the fence. "I'll fix you yet," he promised blood-thirstily as he galloped off, shaking his fist at me.

"Who do you suppose he was?" wondered Lattimer, kinda shaky, and I says, "What the hell does it matter? Forgit the incident and help me give Cousin Bearfield his medicine."

That was easier said than did. Tied up as he was, it was all we could do to get that there elixir down him. I thought I never would get his jaws pried open, using the poker for a lever, but when he opened his mouth to cuss me, we jammed the horn in before he could close it. He left the marks of his teeth so deep on that horn it looked like it'd been in a b'ar-trap.

He kept on heaving and kicking till we'd poured a full dose down him and then he kinda stiffened out and his eyes went glassy. When we taken the horn out his jaws worked but didn't make no sound. But the Perfessor said hosses always acted like that when they'd had a good healthy shot of the remedy, so we left Meshak to watch him, and me and Lattimer went out and sot down on the stoop to rest and cool off.

"Why ain't Meshak onhitched yore buggy?" I ast.

"You mean you expect us to stay here overnight?" says he, aghast.

"Over night, hell!" says I. "You stays till he's kyored, if it takes a year. You may have to make up some more medicine if this ain't enough."

"You mean to say we got to rassle with that maniac three times a day like we just did?" squawked Lattimer.

"Maybe he won't be so vi'lent when the remedy takes holt," I encouraged him. Lattimer looked like he was going to choke, but jest then inside the cabin sounds a yell that even made my hair stand up. Cousin Bearfield had found his voice again.

We jumped up and Meshak come out of the cabin so fast he knocked Lattimer out into the yard and fell over him. The monkey was right behind him streaking it like his tail was on fire.

"Oh, lawdy!" yelled Meshak, heading for the tall timber. "Dat crazy man am bustin' dem ropes like dey was twine. He gwine kill us all, sho'!"

I run into the shack and seen Cousin Bearfield rolling around on the floor and cussing amazing, even for him. And to my horror I seen he'd busted some of the ropes so his left arm was free. I pounced on it, but for a few minutes all I was able to do was jest to hold onto it whilst he throwed me hither and thither around the room with freedom and abandon. At last I kind of wore him down and got his arm tied again jest as Lattimer run in and done a snake dance all over the floor.

"Meshak's gone," he howled. "He was so scared he run off with the monkey and my buggy and team. It's all your fault."

Being too winded to argy I jest heaved Bearfield up on the bunk and staggered over and sot down on the other'n, whilst the Perfessor pranced and whooped and swore I owed him for his buggy and team.

"Listen," I said when I'd got my wind back. "I spent all my money for that elixir, but when Bearfield recovers his reason he'll be so grateful he'll be glad to pay you hisself. Now forgit sech sordid trash as money and devote yore scientific knowledge to gittin' Bearfield sane."

"Sane!" howls Bearfield. "Is that what yo're doin'--tyin' me up and pizenin' me? I've tasted some awful muck in my life, but I never drempt nothin' could taste as bad as that stuff you poured down me. It plumb paralyzes a man. Lemme loose, dammit."

"Will you be ca'm if I onties you?" I ast.

"I will," he promised heartily, "jest as soon as I've festooned the surroundin' forest with yore entrails!"

"Still vi'lent," I said sadly. "We better keep him tied, Perfessor."

"But I'm due to git married in High Horse right now!" Bearfield yelled, giving sech a convulsive heave that he throwed hisself clean offa the bunk. It was his own fault, and they warn't no use in him later blaming me because he hit his head on the floor and knocked hisself stiff.

"Well," I said, "at least we'll have a few minutes of peace and quiet around here. Help me lift him back on his bunk."

"What's that?" yelped the Perfessor, jumping convulsively as a rifle cracked out in the bresh and a bullet whined through the cabin.

"That's probably Droopin' Whiskers," I says, lifting Cousin Bearfield. "I thought I seen a Winchester on his saddle. Say, it's gittin' late. See if you cain't find some grub in the kitchen. I'm hungry."

Well, the Perfessor had an awful case of the willies, but we found some bacon and beans in the shack and cooked 'em and et 'em, and fed Bearfield, which had come to when he smelt the grub cooking. I don't think Lattimer enjoyed his meal much because every time a bullet hit the shack he jumped and choked on his grub. Drooping Whiskers was purty persistent, but he was so far back in the bresh he wasn't doing no damage. He was a rotten shot anyhow. All of his bullets was away too high, as I p'inted out to Lattimer, but the Perfessor warn't happy.

I didn't dare untie Bearfield to let him eat, so I made Lattimer set by him and feed him with a knife, and he was scairt and shook so he kept spilling hot beans down Bearfield's collar, and Bearfield's langwidge was awful to hear.

Time we got through it was long past dark, and Drooping Whiskers had quit shooting at us. As it later appeared, he'd run out of ammunition and gone to borrow some ca'tridges from a ranch house some miles away. Bearfield had quit cussing us, he jest laid there and glared at us with the most horrible expression I ever seen on a human being. It made Lattimer's hair stand up.

But Bearfield kept working at his ropes and I had to examine 'em every little while and now and then put some new ones on him. So I told Lattimer we better give him another dose, and when we finally got it down him, Lattimer staggered into the kitchen and collapsed under the table and I was as near wore out myself as a Elkins can get.

But I didn't dare sleep for fear Cousin Bearfield would get loose and kill me before I could wake up. I sot down on the other bunk and watched him and after while he went to sleep and I could hear the Perfessor snoring out in the kitchen.

About midnight I lit a candle and Bearfield woke up and said, "Blast yore soul, you done woke me up out of the sweetest dream I ever had. I drempt I was fishin' for sharks off Mustang Island."

"What's sweet about that?" I ast.

"I was usin' you for bait," he said. "Hey, what you doin'?"

"It's time for yore dose," I said, and then the battle started. This time he got my thumb in his mouth and would ondoubtedly have chawed it off if I hadn't kind of stunned him with the iron skillet. Before he could recover hisself I had the elixir down him with the aid of Lattimer which had been woke up by the racket.

"How long is this going on?" Lattimer ast despairingly. "Ow!"

It was Drooping Whiskers again. This time he'd crawled up purty clost to the house and his first slug combed the Perfessor's hair.

"I'm a patient man but I've reached my limit," I snarled, blowing out the candle and grabbing a shotgun off the wall. "Stay here and watch Bearfield whilst I go out and hang Droopin' Whiskers' hide to the nearest tree."

I snuck out of the cabin on the opposite side from where the shot come from, and begun to sneak around in a circle through the bresh. The moon was coming up, and I knowed I could out-Injun Drooping Whiskers. Any Bear Creek man

21

could. Sure enough, purty soon I slid around a clump of bushes and seen him bending over behind a thicket whilst he took aim at the cabin with a Winchester. So I emptied both barrels into the seat of his britches and he give a most amazing howl and jumped higher'n I ever seen a bow-legged feller jump, and dropped his Winchester and taken out up the trail toward the north.

I was determined to run him clean off the range this time, so I pursued him and shot at him every now and then, but the dern gun was loaded with bird-shot and all the shells I'd grabbed along with it was the same. I never seen a white man run like he did. I never got clost enough to do no real damage to him, and after I'd chased him a mile or so he turned off into the bresh, and I soon lost him.

Well, I made my way back to the road again, and was jest fixing to step out of the bresh and start down the road toward the cabin, when I heard hosses coming from the north. So I stayed behind a bush, and purty soon a gang of men come around the bend, walking their hosses, with the moonlight glinting on Winchesters in their hands.

"Easy now," says one. "The cabin ain't far down the road. We'll ease up and surround it before they know what's happenin'."

"I wonder what that shootin' was we heered a while back?" says another'n kind of nervous.

22

"Maybe they was fightin' amongst theirselves," says yet another'n. "No matter. We'll rush in and settle the big feller's hash before he knows what's happenin'. Then we'll string Buckner up."

"What you reckon they kidnaped Buckner for?" some feller begun, but I waited for no more. I riz up from behind the bushes and the hosses snorted and reared.

"Hang a helpless man because he licked you in a fair fight, hey?" I bellowed, and let go both barrels amongst 'em.

THEY WAS RIDING SO clost-grouped don't think I missed any of 'em. The way they hollered was disgusting to hear. The hosses was scairt at the flash and roar right in their faces and they wheeled and bolted, and the whole gang went thundering up the road a dern sight faster than they'd come. I sent a few shots after 'em with my pistols, but they didn't shoot back, and purty soon the weeping and wailing died away in the distance. A fine mob they turned out to be!

But I thought they might come back, so I sot down behind a bush where I could watch the road from Gallego. And the first thing I knowed I went to sleep in spite of myself.

When I woke up it was jest coming daylight. I jumped up and grabbed my guns, but nobody was in sight. I guess them Gallego gents had got a bellyful. So I headed back for the cabin and when I got there the corral was empty and the chuck wagon was gone!

I started on a run for the shack and then I seen a note stuck on the corral fence. I grabbed it. It said--

Dear Elkins:

This strain is too much for me. I'm getting white-haired sitting and watching this devil laying there glaring at me, and wondering all the time how soon he'll bust loose. I'm pulling out. I'm taking the chuck wagon and team in payment for my rig that Meshak ran off with. I'm leaving the elixir but I doubt if it'll do Buckner any good. It's for locoed critters, not homicidal maniacs.

Respectfully yours.

Horace J. Lattimer, Esquire.

"Hell's fire," I said wrathfully, starting for the shack.

I dunno how long it had took Bearfield to wriggle out of his ropes. Anyway he was laying for me behind the door with the iron skillet and if the handle hadn't broke off when he lammed me over the head with it he might of did me a injury.

I dunno how I ever managed to throw him, because he fit like a frothing maniac, and every time he managed to break loose from me he grabbed a jug of Lattimer's Loco Elixir and busted it over my head. By the time I managed to stun him with a table laig he'd busted every jug on the place, the floor was swimming in elixir, and my clothes was soaked in it. Where they wasn't soaked with blood.

I fell on him and tied him up again and then sot on a bunk and tried to get my breath back and wondered what in hell to do. Because here the elixir was all gone and I didn't have no way of treating Bearfield and the Perfessor had run off with the chuck wagon so I hadn't no way to get him back to civilization.

Then all at onst I heard a train whistle, away off to the west, and remembered that the track passed through jest a few miles to the south. I'd did all I could for Bearfield, only thing I could do now was to get him back to his folks where they could take care of him.

I run out and whistled for Cap'n Kidd and he busted out from around the corner of the house where he'd been laying for me, and tried to kick me in the belly before I could get ready for him, but I warn't fooled. He's tried that trick too many times. I dodged and give him a good bust in the nose, and then I throwed the bridle and saddle on him, and brung Cousin Bearfield out and throwed him across the saddle and headed south.

That must of been the road both Meshak and Lattimer taken when they run off. It crossed the railroad track about three miles from the shack. The train had been whistling for High Horse when I first heard it. I got to the track before it come into sight. I flagged it and it pulled up and the train crew jumped down and wanted to know what the hell I was stopping them for.

"I got a man here which needs medical attention," I says. "It's a case of temporary insanity. I'm sendin' him back to Texas."

"Hell," says they, "this train don't go nowheres near Texas."

"Well," I says, "you unload him at Dodge City. He's got plenty of friends there which will see that he gits took care of. I'll send word from High Horse to his folks in Texas tellin' 'em to go after him."

So they loaded Cousin Bearfield on, him being still unconscious, and I give the conductor his watch and chain and pistol to pay for his fare. Then I headed along the track for High Horse.

When I got to High Horse I tied Cap'n Kidd nigh the track and started for the depot when who should I run smack into but Old Man Mulholland who immejitly give a howl like a hungry timber wolf.

"Whar's the grub, you hoss-thief?" he yelled before I could say nothing.

"Why, didn't Lem Campbell bring it out to you?" I ast.

"I never seen a man by that name," he bellered. "Whar's my fifty bucks?"

"Heck," I says, "he looked honest."

"Who?" yowled Old Man Mulholland. "Who, you polecat?"

"Lem Campbell, the man I give the dough to for him to buy the grub," I says. "Oh, well, never mind. I'll work out the fifty."

The Old Man looked like he was fixing to choke. He gurgled, "Where's my chuck wagon?"

"A feller stole it," I said. "But I'll work that out too."

"You won't work for me," foamed the Old Man, pulling a gun. "Yo're fired. And as for the dough and the wagon, I takes them out of yore hide here and now."

Well, I taken the gun away from him, of course, and tried to reason with him, but he jest hollered that much louder, and got his knife out and made a pass at me. Now it always did irritate me for somebody to stick a knife in me, so I taken it away from him and throwed him into a nearby hoss trough. It was one of these here V-shaped troughs which narrers together at the bottom, and somehow his fool head got wedged and he was about to drown.

Quite a crowd had gathered and they tried pulling him out by the hind laigs but his feet was waving around in the air so wild that every time anybody tried to grab him they got spurred in the face. So I went over to the trough and taken hold of the sides and tore it apart. He fell out and spit up maybe a gallon of water. And the first words he was able to say he accused me of trying to drownd him on purpose, which shows how much gratitude people has got.

But a man spoke up and said, "Hell, the big feller didn't do it on purpose. I was right here and I seen it all."

And another'n said, "I seen it as good as you did, and the big feller did try to drownd him, too!"

"Air you callin' me a liar?" said the first feller, reaching for his gun.

But jest then another man chipped in and said, "I dunno what the argyment's about, but I bet a dollar you're both wrong!"

And then some more fellers butted in and everybody started cussing and hollering till it nigh deefened me. Someone else reaches for a gun and I seen that as soon as one feller shoots another there is bound to be trouble so I started to gentle the first feller by hitting him over the head. The next thing I know someone hollers at me, "You big hyener!", and tries to ruint me with a knife. Purty soon there is hitting and shooting all over the town. High Horse is sure on a rampage.

I jest had finished blunting my Colts on a varmit's haid when I thinks disgustedly, "Heck, Elkins, you came to this town on a mission of good will! You got business to do. You got yore poor family to think about."

I started to go on to the depot but I heard a familiar voice screech above the racket. "There he is, Sheriff! Arrest the dern' claim-jumper!"

I whirled around quick and there was Drooping Whiskers, a saddle blanket wropped around him like a Injun and walking purty spraddle-legged. He was p'inting at me and hollering like I'd did something to him.

Everybody else quieted down for a minute, and he hollered, "Arrest him, dern him. He throwed me out of my own cabin and ruint my best pants with my own shotgun. I been to Knife River and come back several days quicker'n I aimed to, and there this big hyener was in charge of my shack. He was too dern big for me to handle, so I come to High Horse after the sheriff--soon as I got three or four hundred bird-shot picked out my hide."

"What you got to say about this?" ast the sheriff, kinda uncertain, like he warn't enjoying his job for some reason or other.

"Why, hell," I says disgustedly. "I throwed this varmint out of a cabin, sure, and later peppered his anatomy with bird-shot. But I was in my rights. I was in a cabin which had been loaned me by a man named Lem Campbell--"

"Lem Campbell!" shrieked Drooping Whiskers, jumping up and down so hard he nigh lost the blanket he was wearing instead of britches. "That wuthless critter ain't

29

got no cabin. He was workin' for me till I fired him jest before I started for Knife River, for bein' so triflin'."

"Hell's fire!" I says, shocked. "Ain't there no honesty any more? Shucks, stranger, it looks like the joke's on me."

At this Drooping Whiskers collapsed into the arms of his friends with a low moan, and the sheriff says to me uncomfortably, "Don't take this personal, but I'm afeared I'll have to arrest you, if you don't mind--"

Jest then a train whistled away off to the east, and somebody said, "What the hell, they ain't no train from the east this time of day!"

Then the depot agent run out of the depot waving his arms and yelling, "Git them cows off'n the track! I jest got a flash from Knife River, the train's comin' back. A maniac named Buckner busted loose and made the crew turn her around at the switch. Order's gone down the line to open the track all the way. She's comin' under full head of steam. Nobody knows where Buckner's takin' her. He's lookin' for some relative of his'n!"

There was a lot of noise comin' down that track and all of it waren't the noise that a steam-ingine makes by itself. No, that noise was a different noise all right. That noise was right familiar to me. It struck a chord in my mind and made me wonder kinda what happened to them trainmen.

"Can that be Bearfield Buckner?" wondered a woman. "It sounds like him. Well, if it is, he's too late to git Ann Wilkins."

"What?" I yelled. "Is they a gal in this town named Ann Wilkins?"

"They was," she snickered. "She was to marry this Buckner man yesterday, but he never showed up, and when her old beau, Lem Campbell, come along with fifty dollars he'd got some place, she up and married him and they lit out for San Francisco on their honeymoon--Why, what's the matter, young man? You look right green in the face. Maybe it's somethin' you et--"

It weren't nothin' I et. It was the thoughts I was thinkin'. Here I had gone an' ruint Cousin Bearfield's whole future. And outa kindness. Thet's what busted me wide open. I had ruint Cousin Bearfield's future out of kindness. My motives had been of the loftiest, I had tried to kyore an hombre what was loco from goin' locoer yet, and what was my reward? What was my reward? Jest thet moment I looks up and I seen a cloud of smoke a puffin' down the track and they is a roarin' like the roarin' of a herd of catamounts.

"Here she comes around the bend," yelled somebody. "She's burnin' up the track. Listen at that whistle. Jest bustin' it wide open."

But I was already astraddle of Cap'n Kidd and traveling. The man which says I'm scairt of Bearfield is a liar. A Elkins

31

fears neither man, beast nor Buckner. But I seen that Lem Campbell had worked me into getting Bearfield out of his way, and if I waited till Bearfield got there, I'd have to kill him or get killed, and I didn't crave to do neither.

I headed south jest to save Cousin Bearfield's life, and I didn't stop till I was in Durango. Let me tell you the revolution I got mixed up in there was a plumb restful relief after my association with Cousin Bearfield.

www.ingramcontent.com/pod-product-compliance
Lightning Source LLC
Chambersburg PA
CBHW030242180626
46810CB00008B/3252